Hazy BLOOM AND THE
MYSTERY NEXT DOOR
T
Jennifer Hamburg
pictures by
Jenn Harney
FARRAR STRAUS GIROUX · NEW YORK

SQUARE
FISH

An imprint of Macmillan Publishing Group, LLC
120 Broadway, New York, NY 10271
mackids.com

Our books may be purchased in bulk for promotional, educational, or
business use. Please contact your local bookseller or the Macmillan
Corporate and Premium Sales Department at (800) 221-7945 ext. 5442
or by email at MacmillanSpecialMarkets@macmillan.com.

Library of Congress Cataloging-in-Publication Data

Names: Hamburg, Jennifer, author. | Harney, Jenn, illustrator.
Title: Hazy Bloom and the mystery next door / Jennifer Hamburg ;
    pictures by Jenn Harney.
Description: New York : Farrar Straus Giroux, 2019. | Summary:
    "When Hazy Bloom gets a tomorrow vision of a ghost flying around
    in the empty house next door, her boring summer vacation suddenly
    takes a mysterious, thrilling, and hilariously Hazy-like turn"—
    Provided by publisher.
Identifiers: LCCN 2018011234 | ISBN 978-1-250-23327-1 (paperback) |
    ISBN 978-0-37430-502-4 (ebook)
Subjects: | CYAC: Extrasensory perception—Fiction. | Haunted
    houses—Fiction. | Family life—Fiction. | Humorous stories.
Classification: LCC PZ7.H1756 Ham 2019 | DDC [Fic]—dc23
LC record available at https://lccn.loc.gov/2018011234

Originally published in the United States by Farrar Straus Giroux
First Square Fish edition, 2020
Book designed by Elizabeth H. Clark
Square Fish logo designed by Filomena Tuosto

10 9 8 7 6 5 4 3 2 1

AR: 3.0 / LEXILE: 770L

For those who bravely face their fears
(ghosts and otherwise) and those who make
the winged-monkey kind of role
the most fascinating character in the play
—Jen

For Amelia (she waited her turn)
and Ellowyn and Orson
(who will be able to read this eventually)
—Jenn

MYSTERY
NEXT DOOR

2:55 . . . 2:55 . . . 2:55 . . . It was Friday afternoon, I was sitting at my desk in my classroom, and for

the last several moments I'd been staring at a broken clock. At least, it seemed like it was broken. Because no matter how long I focused on the minute hand, it wasn't budging. And it was very important that it budged. Because today was the last day of school

before summer vacation, and that meant in five minutes there would be no homework, no

spelling quizzes, and no more pointless word problems like

If Sally hiked for 3.2 miles and Jacob hiked for 1.7 miles, how many miles did they hike altogether? (Answer: 4.9 miles and a suggestion that they go ziplining instead.) The point is, the clock was definitely broken because it still said 2:55.

I sighed and slumped down in my seat. I guessed it was like my mom always said: *A watched pot never cooks spaghetti the right way.* Or something like that. Maybe it was about rice.

The minute hand lurched forward to 2:56. Finally! Now we were getting somewhere. I fixed my eyes on the clock and was prepared to stare at it for four more minutes without blinking when I was rudely interrupted by my teacher, Mrs. Agnes.

"And, Hazel Bloom, what are *your* plans for the summer?"

She was eyeing me from the front of the

classroom, along with everyone else. Apparently, while I'd been busy staring at the clock my classmates had been going around the room sharing their summer plans. I was not expecting this question, especially because I hadn't worked out the details of my summer plans just yet. Luckily, I have a talent for being quick on my feet.

"Uhhhhhhhhhhhhh," I said.

Okay, maybe not *that* quick on my feet.

"She's probably just going to hang around her house and do weird stuff like she always does," said a voice behind me. That voice belonged to Luke, and if you think he sounded  annoying, you'd be right. This is why I call him

Mapefrl, which stands for "most annoying person ever, for real live." Mapefrl has been in my class since kindergarten. He's loud, he's rude, and as you can tell, he's extremely immature. Which is why I started arguing with him on the spot.

"Not true!" I countered. "I have big plans for this summer. BIG PLANS."

"Ooh, what are they?" Mrs. Agnes trilled, as if these amazing plans might include her.

I searched my brain for a reasonable-sounding itinerary. "First, we will be going mountain-climbing on Machu Picchu," I began. "Then to the Sahara Desert for a safari. And then if we survive that, we're scheduled to attend the wedding of a wealthy prince in a faraway country."

"Yeah, right," Mapefrl snickered. "What country?"

I quickly scanned the classroom, my eyes landing on Mrs. Agnes's desk.

"Stapler-arctica."

"That's not even real!" he said.

"Is too!"

"Is not!"

"Is too!"

Do you see what I mean? So immature (him, not me). The point is, Mapefrl kicked the back of my chair, I fired a spitball at him, and Mrs. Agnes demanded we both come up to the front of the room immediately. I braced myself for one more round of getting in trouble before school was over.

Then the dismissal bell rang.

Woohoo!

Suddenly, Mrs. Agnes's stern demeanor melted away. "Goodbye, children. Have a wonderful summer!" she called out as we packed up our things. "Don't forget to read! Keep learning! And if anyone wants to come in over the summer for extra worksheets, just—"

"Bye, Mrs. Agnes! See you next year!" I waved. Then I ran toward the door, where Elizabeth was waiting.

2

We were standing at the edge of the school's front lawn when Elizabeth gave the signal.

"Three . . . two . . . one . . . go!"

At the exact same time we dropped our backpacks, got a running start, and began cartwheeling across the grass. This was something I'd call a "tradition," because we did it on the last day of school every single year. It was also something I'd call "not allowed," because every time we began our cartwheeling celebration, we were immediately chased off the lawn by the school principal, whom I believe a) should have been in her office working instead of outside wagging her finger at us, and b) clearly did not appreciate solid gymnastic skills.

Still, we had gotten in a good fifteen cartwheels between the two of us before we were shooed away. We grabbed our backpacks and skedaddled to the bus, huffing and puffing and cracking up at our crazy last minutes of the school year. And there was no one I'd rather have these crazy last minutes with, because Elizabeth Almeida is my best friend in the entire world. We've known each other since we were born, and we are exactly alike in every way. Except that she loves performing and I don't. And she's extremely organized and I'm not. Also, Elizabeth hates watermelon, while I think it is the most perfect food in the universe. But other than that, totally alike.

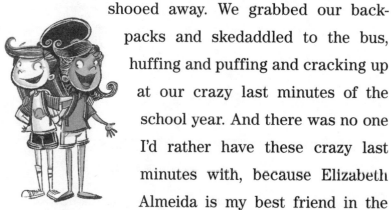

After the bus ride home, we walked down the hill toward our separate streets and gabbed about how much fun this summer was going to be. Elizabeth would be starting theater camp next week (thankfully, it was day camp, so I'd still see her every day). And me? I wasn't actually going to a royal wedding, or on a safari, or to Machu Picchu, but I was still super excited. Because I now officially had a loooong, empty stretch of summer to do anything I wanted. I was free. FREE.

• • • • •

I. Was. So. Bored.

Sooooooooo bored.

I mean, don't get me wrong. The first full day of summer break started out great. I woke up early and took my dog, Mr. Cheese, for a walk. After that, I invented a snack made of cucumbers, pretzels, and Jell-O (surprisingly tasty). Then I washed my hair and dried it with a blow dryer, which I thought turned out very nice—until my baby brother, who we call "The Baby," saw me, pointed, and howled in fear, which I felt was a little overdramatic. Still, it had been a jam-packed, adventurous beginning of summer and I was ready to call it a day. Then I noticed the clock. It was 9:30 in the morning. I called Elizabeth but remembered she was shopping for tap shoes with her mom. What could I do now?

Just then my older brother, Milo (who was the second-most-annoying person after Mapefrl), burst out of his room bouncing a soccer ball on his knee.

"Think fast, Stinkface!" Milo said, faking me out by pretending to toss me the ball only to grab it back to his chest and causing me to duck in panic.

"Ha-ha, very funny. So . . . want to do something?" To be clear, I wouldn't normally choose to interact with such a ridiculously annoying human, but, hey, I was desperate.

"Can't. A bunch of guys are getting together

for a game in the park. See ya, wouldn't want to be ya!"

He pushed past me (annoying!), grabbed a cucumber slice from *my* invented snack (so annoying!), and raced out the door—just as Mom came scurrying down the hallway, her arms full of laundry.

I chased her into her bedroom.

"Mom! Want to play a game?"

Mom dumped the ginormous pile of laundry on her bed. "I'm sorry, Hazel Basil, but I've got to pack. We're leaving the day after tomorrow!"

She was referring to her and Dad's trip to France. They were going for ten days, and my Aunt Jenna was coming to take care of me and Milo and The Baby. Mom's suitcase was sprawled out on her bed, filled to the brim. I'd never been to France, or near France, and didn't know that much about France, but I still think it was worth asking why Mom needed to pack four different pairs of white sneakers. So I did.

She didn't answer and was now muttering about having enough socks, so it was pretty clear she wasn't available to cure my boredom. I thought about finding Dad until I remembered that he was cleaning out the garage. (Also, his idea of fun was teaching me the difference between a skillet and a wok, which is nothing I ever needed to know.)

I went into the living room and called Elizabeth again. No answer.

This was becoming a crisis, as now there was no one left to play with at all.

"Doo-doo!"

I looked down. It was The Baby. He had apparently waddled away from my mom's room during her sock-muttering.

"Doo-doo!" he said again, and plopped down on the floor.

I scrunched up my face, wondering if he was offering to play or telling me he needed a diaper change. I decided it was the first one.

I crouched down to his level, covered my eyes, and then popped them open. "Peekaboo!"

The Baby cracked up so hard, he lost his balance *while sitting on the floor* and knocked into my nose with his extremely hard baby head.

"Ouch!" I grimaced. I was done playing with him.

I delivered The Baby back to my mom then slouched off to the kitchen, where everyone would be able to hear me if I started to literally die from boredom.

I stood in the middle of the floor and sighed loudly. "Soooo bored. Soooooooooooo bored. SOOOOOOOOOO—"

Dad walked in from the garage, tripped over the dog (something he does a lot), and then went to the sink to wash his hands. "If you're that bored, Hazel, I can give you plenty of things to do. Empty the dishwasher, take out the garbage, wash The Baby's bottles . . ."

As I was gasping in horror at these awful ideas, the phone rang. It was Elizabeth, back from shopping *and* calling to announce that she was having a First Day of Summer Sleepover Party. Tonight.

"Woohoo! That's the best news I've heard since sliced bread!"

"That's not the expression, but I'll see you later."

"Cool beans."

I hung up the phone.

Dad was now making himself a bowl of cereal and still going on with his suggested to-do list for me. "Sort the recycling, scrub the downstairs bathroom, scrub the upstairs bathroom—"

"Sorry, I'm going to a sleepover at Elizabeth's!" I called out. I raced to my room before Dad had a chance to point out it was only 9:45 in the morning. I wasn't sure how I'd spend an entire day getting ready for a sleepover, but I was willing to try. Anything to avoid washing The Baby's bottles. Ew, so slobbery.

I was attempting to create a comfortable yet fashion-forward pajama outfit (unicorn nightgown, heart leggings, and fuzzy bunny slippers) when it happened. I suddenly felt prickles and goose bumps, and my skin got hot and cold at the same time. And then an image of a pickle with arms, and the letter *T* flashed through my head. Now, you might be thinking, *Weird, with a cherry on top! Who knows what that's all about, for real live!* But I knew.

It was a tomorrow vision.

3

In the whirlwind of emotion surrounding my first day of summer vacation (utter excitement followed by intense boredom followed by renewed hope and inspiration), I may have forgotten to mention that I have a special ability I call tomorrow power. This means I get visions of things that always come true the next day. Sometimes the visions are perfectly clear, while other times they're as fuzzy as a caterpillar wearing a wool sweater and slippers (not a vision I've ever had but would be very open to). The point is, Elizabeth thinks my special ability means I'm a super-hero, which makes her my sidekick, so, obviously, I needed to tell her about my newest vision ASAP.

When I got to her house, our friends Summer and May were already there. We squealed at the top of our lungs like we hadn't seen each other in years, even though school had ended yesterday. Elizabeth immediately ushered us to her room for pillowcase decorating, and it wasn't until several activities later that I

realized I still hadn't told her about my vision. But whenever I tried to get her alone, she'd get distracted and scamper off somewhere. So, after many unsuccessful attempts, I decided I needed to get her attention in some more creative ways.

This did not go well.

When we were all eating pizza, I was going to whisper to her about my vision, but May squeezed in between us and knocked my pizza slice onto the floor. When we were putting on a talent show I mouthed, "T.P.," for "tomorrow power," but Elizabeth thought I meant "toilet paper" and went to get some new rolls for the bathroom. Later, while we were playing charades, I mimed a clue that I hoped Elizabeth would understand as "I

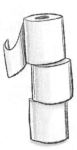

need to talk to you in private, now!" But instead she guessed, "Chicken cutlet robot foot?" which was not even remotely close.

It wasn't until bedtime, as everyone was setting up their sleeping bags, that I finally found Elizabeth by herself. She was in the bathroom brushing her teeth, and while I admit she may have deserved some privacy, I seriously couldn't wait any longer.

"I had a vision!" I whispered to her.

Her reply was hard to understand:

Whfbdbhaifbfuatxth?

Elizabeth realized she still had a bunch of toothpaste in her mouth, spit it out, then asked again.

"What was it?"

I told her about the pickle with arms and the letter *T*.

Like the expert sidekick she was, she thoughtfully wiped her mouth with a towel. "Hmm. That is a tricky one. Maybe you're going to the grocery store for pickles? Or a pickle farm?"

"A pickle farm?"

She gasped. "Maybe it's a pickle *costume* that I'll be wearing for my play at theater camp!"

Personally, I thought this interpretation was a bit of a stretch. But I also understood that even though my tomorrow visions were always super exciting to Elizabeth, there was only one thing on her mind right now, and that was theater camp.

"And then I'll have a pickle tap routine like this!"

I wasn't sure how we got from discussing my tomorrow vision to Elizabeth performing a shuffle-hop-step in her bathroom, but it was obvious I wasn't going to figure anything out tonight.

I applauded her routine (which was actually pretty impressive, considering she did it in socks), then joined my friends on the floor.

Everyone was going around in a circle telling ghost stories, which in my opinion was the very best part of sleepovers.

"Okay, I have one," said Summer, her eyes all mysterious-like. "It's a *true* story about a ghost who lived in an empty house. And whenever someone would walk by, the lights in the house would flicker, and a great big gust of wind would scare people away." She lowered her voice. "One day, a kid decided to get rid of the ghost. That night—when the clock struck midnight—he snuck into the house, all by himself."

I felt my pulse quicken.

"Did he do it? Did he get rid of the ghost?" May asked, her voice squeaky.

Summer paused dramatically. "Yes, he did," she said. "The ghost was never seen or heard from again." She leaned in. "And neither was the kid."

We all gulped.

"Or maybe his family moved to Hawaii. I can't really remember how it ended. But it's totally a true story."

We all burst into giggles. And those giggles

continued for the next hour, until Elizabeth's mom popped her head in and said it was officially bedtime and please no more giggling. Then she left and we giggled some more before one by one we drifted off to sleep.

After an extremely delicious breakfast the next morning (Elizabeth's mom should open up a chocolate chip pancake restaurant, for real

live), I decided it was time to make Big Summer Plans with all of my friends. Don't get me wrong, the sleepover was a great start. But that was just one night. I still had 103 days of summer left to go.

This turned out to be a disaster times eleven million. Because that's when I found out that every one of my friends had their own Big Summer Plans, and none of them involved me. Elizabeth, of course, was going to theater camp. May was visiting her grandparents in Kansas City—which was not in Kansas but in Missouri. And Summer was going to sleepaway camp in Missouri City—which was not in Missouri but in Texas. The point is, I believe these cities should relocate so it isn't so confusing. Also, it was now clear that I had NO ONE to hang out with this summer. Even Mom and Dad were going away on a whirlwind adventure in France. I had been so excited about my Big Summer Plans, but now the only one without plans was me.

When I got back home later that morning, I took Mr. Cheese for a walk and started thinking up ways to feel sorry for myself, given that this was going to be the worst summer ever. As we passed in front of the Thibodeauxs' house, which was next to ours, I wondered if maybe I could hang out with them, until I realized that Mr. and Mrs. Thibodeaux were about eighty years old, so I wasn't sure what activities we'd agree on. Also, I remembered that they went to visit their grandchildren each year for the entire summer, so they weren't around anyway. That must have been why their porch light was on in the middle of the day—so possible burglars would think they were home. The Thibodeauxs may have been old, but you can't say they weren't clever.

Then something strange happened. Out of nowhere, Mr. Cheese started barking like crazy. At first, I couldn't figure out why, but then I noticed the Thibodeauxs' porch light had started flickering on and off. Slowly at first, then faster and faster.

"Hush!" I told Mr. Cheese. "It's just a light." I walked closer to the porch and pointed. "See? A flickering light. No biggie, okay?"

But Mr. Cheese kept barking. I sighed and tugged on his leash to turn around when the porch light flickered on again, and this time I was close enough to see it light up the welcome mat on their doorstep. Now, I don't normally pay attention to welcome mats, but there was something about this one that seemed familiar. It has a giant cactus on it: a large green body with two cactus branches sticking out to each side. I gasped as I recognized what it was. *A pickle with arms.* Right next to the cactus was a giant *T,* for "Thibodeaux." It was my vision!

My first thought was this: Why would anyone have a welcome mat with a cactus on it, since I don't consider cacti very welcoming? My second thought was: Why would I have a vision about the Thibodeauxs? They weren't even home; their house was empty. It didn't make sense, although I was starting to get a gnawing feeling in my belly I couldn't ignore (and I knew

it wasn't hunger because I was still full from all of those chocolate chip pancakes).

Then, out of nowhere, a sudden gust of wind nearly knocked me off my feet.

Mr. Cheese started barking again, and the gnawing feeling returned as I began putting things together in my head. *Empty house. Flickering lights. Sudden gust of wind.* It was exactly like Summer's ghost story. I stood frozen for a moment, staring at the Thibodeauxs' front door. Was it possible? Could there really be . . . ? I shook my head, dismissing the ridiculous thought. There was no way a ghost was living in this house. No way! It was way too crazy.

Or was it?

I ran home and immediately dialed Elizabeth. I was sort of freaking out, but I knew as soon as I told my best friend what had happened she'd say something reassuring like, *You must stay as far away from that house as possible, which may include taking the long way to get to my street or remaining inside all summer.* Frankly, I was open to either of those options.

So you can imagine my surprise when, after I described the cactus welcome mat, the flickering lights, and the unexpected gust of wind, Elizabeth said, "Want to hear my audition song for theater camp?"

Look, I adored Elizabeth, and I knew she cared about me more than anyone else in the world besides her parents and possibly her "boyfriend," Antonio, who is in fifth grade and whom I have never seen her speak to once. But sometimes she could be, well, a little self-centered. So when she ignored my shocking news and instead started singing "Tomorrow" from *Annie*, I cut her off.

"Elizabeth! Did you hear what I said?"

She paused on the other end of the line. "Was it about Antonio?"

"No!"

Elizabeth apologized and asked me to repeat

my story, and this time she gasped as if she finally understood the importance of it all. "Oh my goodness, Hazy Bloom! You know what we need to do, right?"

"Yep. I need to get my family to move to Machu Picchu."

"No. We need to solve the mystery!"

"What?!"

"Look. Your job as a superhero is to prevent doom, right?" she argued. "And what's more doom-y than a ghost!"

She had a point. And she also wasn't done.

"Just think, if you get rid of a ghost, you'll become a local celebrity, which means as your best friend *I'll* become a celebrity, too. I mean, what could be better than that?"

Honestly, in my mind there were a whole lot of things better than being a celebrity, like inventing a secret language to communicate with owls, or watching The Baby try to do a

THE DAILY JOURNAL
LOCAL GIRL PREVENTS DOOM!!!!
ELIZABETH IS HER BEST FRIEND!

somersault. Still, it *would* be pretty cool if word got around I'd gotten rid of a ghost. I'd pretty much become a hero. Maybe I'd even get my picture in the newspaper!

I smiled. It turned out I had Big Summer Plans after all. I was going to get rid of the ghost next door. After I figured out if there really was one.

I hung up the phone, feeling energized. I loved a good mystery, even if it did involve a haunted house and a creepy ghost. Good thing I didn't spook easily.

But then came a voice.

And then a loud, long scream from me.

Okay, it turned out it was just Dad saying hello, but seriously? He came out of *nowhere*.

"Sheesh, Hazy, you look like you just saw a ghost."

"Not yet." I forced a laugh.

Dad arched his eyebrows.

I decided to change the subject. "So what's up?"

Dad threw me his most lovable smile. "Well, I was wondering if my *favorite* daughter would help me pack my suitcase for our trip?"

"I'm your only daughter, but sure, what do you need?" I asked, welcoming the distraction.

"Well first I need . . . my suitcase. It was in the garage yesterday, but now it's disappeared."

Another mystery! For the next million hours, Dad and I searched the entire house for his missing suitcase. You'd think a big old thing like that would be easy to find, but we had to look in three rooms, the very messy attic, and the garage again before Mom returned with The Baby from the playground and announced she'd already gotten it out of his closet and put it on their bed.

I helped Dad gather his list of items, checking them off as we went: shirts, pants, underwear, socks, a toothbrush, a camera, batteries, phone cords, a deck of cards, and a travel-sized back scratcher in case he got itchy.

By lunchtime, Dad was fully packed. He made me a "thanks for helping" grilled cheese

sandwich and an iced sweet tea, and then I headed to my room to work on my newest hobby: backbend writing. I was upside down for several minutes, attempting to write my first name, when I felt the sensation—hot and cold. I gulped. A vision was coming—and it might be about the ghost!

But no vision appeared. It turned out the "hot" was just a nice warm patch of sunlight streaming through my window, and the "cold" was me knocking over the glass of iced tea onto my leg.

It was only after I'd cleaned up my mess and gone downstairs to watch some TV that I got that prickly, goose-bumpy feeling all over. This time, a tomorrow vision appeared for real: of a small, gray, whiskery mouse.

Ew.

A couple of months ago, I really wanted a pet iguana. That didn't quite work out. (It's a long story involving a school fundraiser, a trip to the pet store, and a whole bunch of doggie tutus.) But the point is, even though I didn't get an iguana, I still liked them. They're smart, friendly, and surprisingly cute.

The same cannot be said for mice. They are not geniuses, I don't find them friendly, and they're most certainly not cute. Which is why the next morning, after I woke up, sat on the edge of my bed, and remembered my vision, I yanked my feet up off the floor in pure panic. I scrunched up into a terrified ball, fearfully

scanning my room for the creepy rodent. I didn't know when I'd see it, or where it would be, or if it might bring along any mouse friends, but one thing was for sure: I'd be avoiding the floor for the rest of the day. I figured as long I didn't have to leave my room, that shouldn't be too hard.

"Kids, breakfast!" Mom called from the kitchen.

Well, this was a curve ball. How was I supposed to get to the kitchen without touching the floor? I had an idea. Standing on my bed, I slid my foot over to my nightstand, then onto my desk, then down to my beanbag chair, hopping from one piece of furniture to the next until I managed to get to my bedroom door. I smiled, delighted with my wildly clever thinking.

Then I got to the hallway. There was nothing there but walls and a looooong stretch of floor, which I realize is what a hallway *is*, but it didn't make me feel any better. And I wasn't taking any chances. So when Milo came out of his room and walked past my door, I took a flying leap and landed on his back.

"Piggyback me!" I screeched.

"*HEY!*" Milo yowled, completely taken by surprise.

He tried to wrestle me off him, but I held on tight, like I was on a bucking bronco at the rodeo, as he stumbled down the hallway. (Hey, he should be grateful—at least we didn't have any stairs.) By the time he finally pried me loose, we were already in the kitchen, where, I'm happy to report, there was plenty of furniture to stand on. And they say big brothers are good-for-nothing, stinky armpits! (Actually, I don't know for sure if anyone else says that, but I can confirm that I've said it numerous times.)

Milo turned to me, angrily. "What is wrong with you, Hazy? You could have thrown my back out! I start my soccer clinic this week!"

I apologized and told Milo I appreciated his kindness, and the good news was that I would not need his piggyback services for the rest of the morning. Unfortunately, The Baby had seen us and was now begging for a piggyback ride himself. And what was Milo going to do, reject a

BABY? I giggled as Milo
reluctantly heaved The
Baby onto his back and
galloped around the table,
The Baby squealing in
delight. That's when I caught
Mom looking at me.

"Hazel, why are you standing on the kitchen
table?"

As a reminder, I was still avoiding the floor.

"No reason," I said, untruthfully.

"Then please get down."

"I can't."

"And why not?" Uh-oh. Mom, Dad, and Milo
were now staring up at me, waiting for an
answer. I needed to come clean.

"Um . . . I think . . . there might be . . . a
mouse?"

The next thing that happened was what you
might call "pandemonium." Mom squealed and

jumped up from her chair, knocking over the syrup, which Mr. Cheese starting lapping up. Dad tripped over Mr. Cheese, and Milo slipped on the floor, almost dropping The Baby, who was still on his back. Meanwhile, I stood patiently on the kitchen table watching my family basically go completely bananas.

"Did you find it?" my mom screeched to Dad.

"No!" Dad yelled back. "Hazy, where was it? Where did you see the mouse?"

"Well, I didn't . . . actually . . . *see* it . . . yet."

My entire family stopped and turned to me.

"You didn't see a mouse? They why did you say you did?" Dad asked.

"I didn't say I saw a mouse. I said there might *be* a mouse."

Mom put her hands on her hips and sent her laser glare my way. "Hazel Bloom, is this one of those times where you say you know something, but you won't tell us how you know it, and we don't know if we should believe you, but it causes everyone to go running around looking for a mouse?"

So here's the trickiest part about tomorrow power: Nobody knows. Well, except for me. And Elizabeth. From the very beginning, Elizabeth and I had decided that if I told other people, either they wouldn't believe me, or they'd believe me and proceed to ask me every second of the day what would be happening tomorrow, which would become super annoying, for real live. Since neither of these seemed like good choices, we'd decided it was best to keep it a secret.

This is why I answered Mom's question the following way: "Yuppers."

I was sent to my room for making up stories about a pretend mouse. I didn't even get a piggyback ride there.

7

"Hazy Bloom? What are you doing in our tree?"

It was later that afternoon, my punishment was over, and I was now perched on a branch of the birch tree outside Elizabeth's house. She had just arrived home from her first day at theater camp, and I had come over to greet her. As you might have guessed, I still hadn't found the mouse.

I told her about my vision.

She nodded and then switched the subject immediately. "Guess what play we're doing in theater camp?"

"Hm . . . Is it—"

"Okay, I'll tell you!" she said, then paused for dramatic effect. "*The Wizard of Oz*! And guess what my part is?"

"Uhhh, is it—"

"Okay, I'll tell you!" Another dramatic pause. I was expecting her to say "Dorothy" or "The Scarecrow" or "Glinda the Good Witch," who I admired because she got to travel by bubble, which is obviously a fantastic mode of transportation.

But instead Elizabeth said, "I'm a dancing winged monkey!"

I had nothing to say about that. But Elizabeth did.

"We have rehearsal every day, and then we'll have dress rehearsal and a *tech run*. Do

you know what that means? No, of course you
don't. But trust me, it's very important. And the
monkeys have this really cool dance and I have
a SOLO in it. Isn't that amazing? Yes, yes, it is!"

If you didn't catch that, Elizabeth just asked
and answered her own question, which she
liked to do sometimes. And given all of the
energy I was spending avoiding a mouse, that
was fine with me. She went on for a while, telling me about her rehearsals and costumes and
how it was going to be so much fun.

Then she stopped because I think she'd just

remembered she was speaking to another actual person, me. She glanced at the ground.

"I don't see a mouse, Hazy Bloom. I think you can come down."

"Maybe later."

"You can't stay up there all day! Besides, we need to figure out what your vision means." She paused as if something had just occurred to her. "Maybe it has to do with the ghost next door!"

"What would a mouse have to do with a ghost?"

"It could be his pet."

"Ghosts don't have pets!" I paused. "Do they?"

Elizabeth crossed her arms defiantly. "Well, you're not going to find out by sitting in that tree."

We stared at each other for about ten more seconds before I said, "Fine. I'll come down." It wasn't really that Elizabeth had convinced me of anything. The truth is, my bottom hurt from sitting on that branch for so long. Also, Elizabeth had begun tap-dancing on the sidewalk, so my decision was kind of made for me.

I climbed down from the tree, and Elizabeth and I began discussing how we could locate the mouse from my vision. I suggested setting mousetraps all the way from her house to mine. Elizabeth said we should try to lure the mouse to us with music, like the Pied Piper, which she pointed out would be a lot less gross than catching it in a trap and would also allow her to play her recorder.

In the end, we decided to go to my house, build a fort, and get started on one of the seven businesses we planned to have by tenth grade.

And if we found a mouse along the way, we'd deal with it then.

As we made our way down the sidewalk, I carefully followed each of Elizabeth's footsteps so I was sure not to step on a mouse. This plan

was working well when all of a sudden—just as we were passing the Thibodeauxs' house—a skateboard decorated with a lightning bolt whizzed toward us, and the shock of it sent me tumbling to the ground.

"Hey!" I hollered. I looked up angrily to see who the skateboarder was, and my mouth dropped open in disbelief.

It was Mapefrl.

"What are *you* doing here?" I demanded, offended that he was appearing in my life outside a school setting.

"I'm visiting my uncle. He lives one street over," he replied. "What are YOU doing here?"

"I *live* here. This is *my* street," I said.

"Oh, you *own* it?" he shot back. "Like, you're the *queen* of your street?" He took a snack bag of cheese puffs out of his pocket and started loudly crunching away.

This would be a good time to mention that Mapefrl was clearly just as annoying when we weren't in school.

Elizabeth piped in. "Yes. She's the queen of the street, and she commands you leave at once! Right, Hazy?"

I nodded. "Yes. I command it." Then I added, "At once."

"You can't command me to leave!"

"Oh yes I can!"

Soon we were yelling back and forth, arguing about what a queen does and whether she can actually rule a street, when I suddenly stopped cold. Because that's when I saw something scurrying across the ground.

It looked like a mouse.

I screamed.

Elizabeth screamed.

Then we ran like our lives depended on it, across the Thibodeauxs' lawn and straight into their backyard, where we crouched behind an empty planter. From my  hiding spot I could hear Mapefrl skateboarding away, probably heading back to his uncle's house. I was so freaked out about the mouse, I couldn't even enjoy the fact that he was now gone.

"Do you see it?" I said, looking around in alarm. "The mouse?"

"No, but it could be anywhere!" Elizabeth said back.

We braced ourselves, listening intently for any sign the mouse was nearby. And that's when I heard a completely different noise altogether. A horrible, unsettling rattling sound. It was coming from inside the Thibodeauxs' house. I suddenly realized something even worse than encountering a mouse: being in the Thibodeauxs' backyard meant we were now possibly very close to a ghost.

I heard the rattling again.

"Do you hear that?" I squeaked to Elizabeth.

"Yes—what is it?" she asked, her voice shaking.

"I don't know," I said. I stood up and inched a few steps closer.

"Hazy Bloom, get back here! What if it's the—"

She stopped talking. Because on the ground in front of us, a large, looming shadow appeared. I think we were both too stunned to speak—was it the ghost? Was it right behind us? My heart skipped a beat as the shadow grew bigger and bigger and—

"Doo doo!"

Huh?

I whirled around. Standing behind us, with a bewildered look on his face, was Dad. And The Baby.

"Hazel?"

"Dad?"

"Mr. Bloom?"

"Elizabeth?"

"Squer!" The Baby said.

I followed The Baby's gaze, wondering what a "squer" was. Then I saw it, scampering across the ground and up the side of a tree. It was the same creature I'd seen in front of the house . . . and now I could see that it was a squirrel. Which is not nearly as creepy as a mouse (but a lot more creepy than an iguana, just so we're clear).

61

Relief washed over me as I realized there was no mouse *or* ghost—only Dad, The Baby, and a squirrel. Unfortunately, that relief lasted for about two seconds before the interrogation began. Dad sternly asked me what I was doing in the Thibodeauxs' backyard, and I pointed out that he was in the Thibodeauxs' backyard, too, so I could ask him the same question. This answer did not fly with him, and I was sure he was going to demand that I answer him right this minute or "face the consequences, missy," which was a name he used when he was either a) mad at me or b) forgot my real name.

But instead he said, "Come on home, Hazel. There's someone here to see you."

"There is?" I asked.

Then, I heard, "Yoo-hoo! Hello, Hazy Bloom! It's me, your favorite aunt, here to babysit!" Aunt Jenna stuck her head over the fence that

stood between the Thibodeauxs' house and ours. "I've got presents! I already gave The Baby his. Show Hazy your mousie, sweetie!"

Mousie?

Only then did I notice that The Baby was

holding a new toy. It was a small, plush, whiskery mouse. The very one from my vision.

"Doo doo!" The Baby said gleefully.

I dropped my face into my hands as Elizabeth stifled a giggle.

8

After the Mapefrl-mouse-squirrel fiasco, Elizabeth decided it was probably better if she headed back home. I said goodbye, then followed Dad and The Baby back to our house while I pondered various questions, such as:

1. How can I figure out if there's really a ghost?
2. What was that horrible rattling sound?
3. How did Mapefrl get even more annoying?
4. Why would anyone want a toy mouse?

I didn't get any of these answers, however, because as soon as we stepped through the door, Aunt Jenna grabbed me in a hug.

"We are going to have SO much fun together this week! I can't wait!"

"Me too, I can't wait, too. Yay. Fun," I replied not so enthusiastically.

So here's the thing about Aunt Jenna: I wasn't *totally* bummed she was going to be watching us for the week. After all, Aunt Jenna was a great cook, she'd taught me how to do things like birdcalling and playing a thumb piano, and she liked to have impromptu dance parties, which I would never consider a bad thing. But she was also a little, well, odd. She was always just a little too cheerful, she wore a perfume that made me sneeze, and she had a habit of giving me strange gifts, which brought us back to the current moment.

Aunt Jenna joyfully held out a large, sparkly box. "Open, open, open!" she sang like she was in an opera.

I opened the box to find a polka-dotted bathrobe. I thanked her, even though I was

pretty sure I'd never wear it. What ten-year-old has ever had the need for a bathrobe?

• • • • •

That night, we were having one last dinner together before Mom and Dad left for their trip the following morning. As Dad served his famous lasagna, Mom was rattling off a million last-minute instructions to Aunt Jenna.

"Milo starts his soccer clinic on Wednesday, so make sure he puts on sunscreen every day," she was saying. "And The Baby loves the playground, but don't let him play in the sand too long or he'll start to eat it."

"Got it."

"Oh, and just as a reminder, Hazy likes to argue."

"I do not!" I said.

Aunt Jenna chuckled. "Theresa, we'll be fine."

"You're right," Mom said, waving her hand. "Once I'm on the plane tomorrow I'll start to relax."

Aunt Jenna paused. "You should take earplugs," she said, "just in case there's a baby sitting in the seat right behind you."

"All right," Mom said, nodding.

"Oh, and wear short sleeves in case the air conditioning isn't working."

"Okay . . ."

"And bring a pen, because you might end up sitting next to a nice lady you'd like to exchange a recipe with."

"Jenna, you sure seem to think you know a lot about our plane ride tomorrow!" Mom said with a laugh. I was thinking the same thing. But unlike Mom, I knew why Aunt Jenna was saying all of that stuff.

It was because Aunt Jenna had tomorrow power, too.

How did I know this for sure? I didn't. In fact, I'd even asked her about it one time over the phone, and she'd said she didn't know what I was talking about. But I don't think she was telling the truth. I'm not sure why she hasn't admitted she has tomorrow power or if she ever will. All I know is that she was now telling Mom that she should probably bring a snack because the airplane might be out of peanuts.

Dad stood up and gave a big grin. "In honor of our trip, for dessert I present . . . French vanilla ice cream!"

Okay, that was a nice touch. Everyone started grabbing bowls and spoons, and right as Dad started scooping the ice cream, it happened. I felt the prickles and goose bumps, and my skin got hot and cold at the same time. "Hazy, what toppings do you want?" I vaguely heard Dad ask.

My vision appeared.

"Hazy . . . ? Hello?"

It was a piano, flying through the air, and something else I couldn't quite make out. What *was* that? Then I realized.

"An avocado!" I said.

Dad looked at me. "You want an avocado on your ice cream?"

Oops. I hadn't meant to say that out loud.

I told Dad I was joking of course, and then asked for strawberry syrup and sprinkles. But I caught Aunt Jenna eyeing me with a crooked smile, as if she knew exactly why I'd said that.

After dinner, I continued to practice my backbend writing (I'd moved on from my first to my last name), while also trying to figure out what a flying piano and an avocado could mean. Could they have something to do with the mystery next door? I needed to find out. But how?

When I was done hanging out upside down, I went digging through my closet, where I found an old pair of binoculars I'd gotten for my

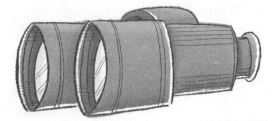

seventh birthday. I'd only used them twice: once for observing a bird's nest outside my window, and once when I tried to look deep inside a Hostess cupcake. I didn't think I'd have a use for them again, but now I realized they would be perfect for one thing in particular.

Ghost-spying.

The next morning, I walked Mom and Dad out to the waiting taxi.

"Have fun in France! *Bonjour! Merci!* Chocolate croissant!" I said, giving them big hugs.

Milo pointed out that none of those words meant "goodbye" in French, but Mom and Dad didn't seem to mind.

"We'll see you next week!" Dad said.

"We love you!" Mom added.

After one more round of hugs, they got into the taxi and headed off to the airport.

As I watched them go, I felt a little pang of sadness. I was going to miss them. But at least I had a busy day ahead of me to keep my mind off that. I turned and beelined for my room to begin a full day of ghost-spying.

I'd been staring through my binoculars for approximately six minutes (and had so far only

discovered some dried filling from a Hostess cupcake on one of the lenses) when Aunt Jenna knocked on my door.

"Hazy Bloom?" she called.

"Busy!" I said back.

But Aunt Jenna did not take the hint, because instead of walking away, she threw open my door and practically waltzed into my room. "Yes, we WILL be busy. Because for our first full day together, I have planned a Fantastic Day of Fun! Whaddaya say?"

"No, thank you, I have plans," I replied, not adding that those plans involved investigating a flying piano, an avocado, and possibly a ghost that might or might not be haunting the house next door. The point is, Aunt Jenna didn't seem to care what my plans were, because twenty minutes later I found myself piled into Mom's car along with Milo and The Baby, heading off to do a whole bunch of stuff I didn't want to do.

Also, just to be perfectly clear, Aunt Jenna's Fantastic Day of Fun was neither fantastic nor fun. It was an epic fail.

First, we went to the local merry-go-round, and after the ride was over The Baby spit up on my sandal.

Then we went to lunch, where I ordered a hamburger with pickles but they messed up and gave me a hot dog with onions.

Then Milo spotted a video game store, so we went in there for like a million and a half hours and I almost passed out from boredom, for real live.

Then on the way back to the car, I got three mosquito bites.

By the time we got home, it was already getting dark, my mosquito bites were itching like crazy, and I was sure I'd missed the chance to see any evidence of the ghost.

I was sitting on the front steps drowning my sorrows in a glass of chocolate milk when I heard the same *whooshing* sound from yesterday. It was Mapefrl, back on his lightning skateboard. He was munching on cheese puffs again.

Just great.

"Don't you have anywhere better to skate?" I inquired.

"This street is the smoothest," he said with a shrug.

"Well, I know *that*," I replied, even though I'd never noticed any such thing. I tried to ignore him while he rudely continued skateboarding around *my* cul-de-sac, but it was difficult since he kept saying things like "Check this out!" and "Watch this one!" and "Look at this!"

Finally, I told him I was going inside.

"Suit yourself," he said, and continued to skate. But just as he passed in front of the Thibodeauxs' house, Mapefrl suddenly lost his balance and stumbled from his skateboard and fell onto the grass.

"Whoa!" he said.

"Hey! Are you okay?" I asked, running over to him. I mean, I still thought he was annoying, but I wasn't heartless.

He jumped up and brushed off his pant leg.

"Yeah. But that was weird. I never fall like that. It just happened out of nowhere."

Not nowhere, I realized with dread. *In front of the Thibodeauxs' house.*

If that wasn't a sign of a ghost, I didn't know what was.

Mapefrl hopped back on his skateboard and headed down the street back to his uncle's,

leaving me standing in front of the neighbors' house by myself. And since I hadn't seen anything yet resembling a flying piano or an avocado, *and* had just gotten more evidence of a ghost, I made a decision right then and there.

I took a deep breath and walked toward the Thibodeauxs' front porch.

The porch light was flickering again, and now that it was dark it looked a lot more spooky. I climbed the front steps and glanced in both directions. Did I really want to do this? I decided yes. If I saw a flying piano in the house, then I'd know for sure there was a ghost in there. It would be my proof! I just needed to find the perfect window to peek through . . .

Darn. The windows were covered by shutters, so I couldn't see in. Then I noticed a broken slat way high up on one of the shutters. I could climb onto the window ledge and then peek through there.

I propped one foot on the ledge and hauled myself up, frustrated that I was wearing flip-flops instead of more reliable window-climbing shoes. Now I was standing up high, and once I steadied myself, I peeked through the broken slat. The good news was that I could see everything in the front room. The bad news? None of those things was a flying piano. Maybe the piano was in the next room over? I tilted my body a little more, just to see around the wall . . .

All of a sudden, I heard a SLAM—from inside the house. I was so startled, I lost my balance.

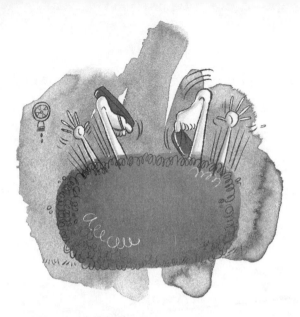

I screeched as I fell off the ledge and into the bushes below. After checking to make sure I hadn't sprained my ankle, broken my arm, or gotten any thorns in my butt, I quickly looked around to make sure no one had seen me—not only because I was peeking into someone's house, but because if anyone witnessed that fall it would be totally embarrassing, for real live.

I spotted a knob close by and grabbed it to pull myself up. What I didn't realize is that on my way up I accidentally turned it. Suddenly, about ten sprinkler heads sprang to life, and water started spraying all over the lawn, and all over me. So you see I really had no choice but to start screaming my head off.

I sputtered and snatched at the knob, finally managing to turn it and the sprinklers back

off. Meanwhile, Aunt Jenna must have heard the commotion, because she ran out of our house holding The Baby and rushed over to me.

The Baby looked at me oddly, then grinned in delight. "Yay!" he said, as if celebrating the fact that I now looked like a drowned rat (which is even worse than a mouse).

"Hazy Bloom, what in the world happened?" Aunt Jenna cried.

I knew I needed a convincing explanation, and usually I was pretty good at coming up with these kinds of things (you might remember my story about Stapler-arctica). But I think my brain was waterlogged.

"Well, Aunt Jenna, see, I was trying to get a good look at the Thibodeauxs' greenery,

because . . . I've become very interested in, um, gardening."

She tilted her head at me. "Gardening?"

"Yep. Gardening. I mean, how does it all work? The grass . . . the trees . . . the flowers. It's just fascinating!"

Aunt Jenna nodded slowly. Then she told me it was time to come home.

As I walked—cold, wet, and shivering—I fended off The Baby, who was currently trying to squeeze water from my shorts. Talk about embarrassing.

A few minutes later, I was sitting on the couch, wrapped in the polka-dotted bathrobe Aunt Jenna had given me. And I've got to admit—it felt heavenly. It was like wearing a big, soft, polka-dotted cloud. I guess it had come in handy after all. Like all of her other gifts.

"Okay, kids," Aunt Jenna said, calling over Milo. "I have one more surprise planned for our Fantastic Day of Fun!"

Great, I thought. *What's it going to be now? Mr. Cheese peeing in my shoe?*

"We're watching a movie!"

I was in no mood for a movie, but I was too warm and dry now to relocate. I reached for my (new) glass of chocolate milk and took a sip, just as the movie was starting. I didn't even know what the movie was called, but I do know this: in the first frame, a piano flew across a white backdrop. That's right. A flying piano. I was so surprised, I spit out my chocolate milk.

Aunt Jenna handed me a napkin as she set out a snack. Chips and some kind of green dip.

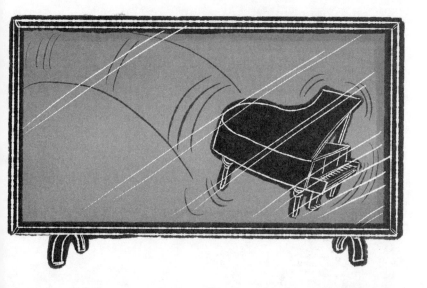

"This is really good. What's in it?" Milo asked, scooping some dip onto a chip.

All of a sudden, I knew what she was going to say. So I said it for her. "Avocados," I barely whispered.

"That's right!" Aunt Jenna exclaimed.

I sank deeper into the couch.

11

The next morning, I was finishing the maze on the back of my cereal box when Aunt Jenna told me she had a surprise for me.

"Really? What is it?" I asked.

"If I told you, it wouldn't be a surprise, silly! Now, go get dressed and meet me at the car."

After our Fantastic Day of Fun, which I had secretly renamed the Dreadful Day of Doom, I couldn't imagine a surprise from Aunt Jenna being all that wonderful. Plus, I was incredibly frustrated that my vision had nothing to do with the mystery next door and everything to do with a movie about a piano (which was actually pretty entertaining, but that's totally beside the point).

Still, my curiosity got the best of me. Before long, I had gotten dressed, brushed my teeth, fed my fish, tried to make a natural-looking messy bun, failed at the messy bun and made pigtails instead, and then searched all over the house for my left shoe, which *someone* (I'm looking at you, The Baby!) had put in the bathtub. Meanwhile, during all of this rigmarole, I had narrowed down Aunt Jenna's surprise to three possibilities:

1. We were going to a ghost investigation ceremony, where I'd learn that I'd been right all along and was being honored with a medal.

2. We were going to a secret location where Aunt Jenna was finally going to tell me she had tomorrow power, at

which time we'd create a master plan to destroy the enemy (enemy to be determined).

3. We were going to the aquarium.

I would have been happy with any of these things, so imagine my surprise when—of all the places in the entire city of Denver and the surrounding world—Aunt Jenna drove down the street, through our neighborhood, and into the parking lot of my school.

"Surprise!" she trilled, getting out of the car and opening my door.

I looked around. "What are we doing here?"

"Well, it turns out your school is planting a brand-new vegetable garden over the summer. And since you mentioned a love of gardening, I signed you up as a volunteer!"

She what?

"Isn't it exciting!"

I could not believe this. First, I come up empty finding a ghost, and now I had to spend time at school? *In the summer?* This was the worst! Then it got more worse.

"Hazel Bloom? What a surprise!"

Slowly, I turned around to see who it was, even though there was no mistaking that shrill, high-pitched voice.

It was Mrs. Agnes.

• • • • •

It turned out Mrs. Agnes was an enthusiastic gardener, so when the school decided to plant a garden, she was the first one they called. She was thrilled that I was there to help, but also a little surprised because they hadn't announced the garden yet. There was going to be an article about it in the newspaper tomorrow morning, she said, so it was strange that I even knew about it. But I knew how we knew.

I turned to my aunt pointedly. "Yes, Aunt Jenna. How *did* we know about the garden?"

"Oh, a little birdie told me," Aunt Jenna said, cool as a cucumber.

I was about to argue that the "birdie" was really a "tomorrow vision" and that this "garden" was really "a way for Aunt Jenna to force me to go to school in the summer and be miserable." The point is, Mrs. Agnes interrupted my thoughts by giving me an ugly pair of work gloves and then shoving a rake in my hands.

"Let's get going! You're in charge of arugula."

"Who's Arugula?" I asked, glancing around.

Mrs. Agnes burst into giggles. "It's not a person—it's an herb! And these seedlings aren't going to plant themselves. Follow me!"

Two hours later, I had decided this was the worst summer vacation ever since summer vacations began (which I believe was in the year 1829). And we were only five days in.

12

I dragged my feet into my house and flopped onto the couch facedown.

"Why don't you go relax in your room for a while before dinner?" Aunt Jenna asked.

"Nnnnnnnn," I replied, too tired to say an actual word. We had just gotten back from school, and I was in no mood to talk, much less

move. My hands were blistered from using the rake to loosen the soil, my clothes were covered in dirt, I smelled like arugula, and I'm pretty sure a pebble had made its way into my under-wear.

"Was it even a little bit fun?" she asked.

"No," I said. I managed to push myself upright and told Aunt Jenna that it was incredi-bly cruel to torture a small child like me by sending her out into the hot sun to work in a garden for an *entire day.*

"It was two hours."

"Well, it felt a lot longer," I said stubbornly. And then Aunt Jenna told me it would seem shorter tomorrow.

Tomorrow? I was going back?

I flopped back down. I needed to call Eliza-beth and share how badly my life was going.

Of course that would mean standing up and walking to the phone. Luckily, at that very moment the phone rang and Aunt Jenna handed it to me.

"Hi!" Elizabeth chirped.

In spite of my exhaustion, I smiled. Do you see how in sync we are? Just when I was about to call her, she beat me to it!

After describing her winged-monkey dance in great detail, she turned her attention to me—and the ghost investigation. "So?" she asked eagerly. "Did you see anything weird today?"

"Yes," I replied. "Mrs. Agnes."

13

It was two days later, and I'm sorry to report
that my summer had not improved one bit. In
fact, it was still as miserable as ever, because at
the moment I was pushing a wheelbarrow filled
with manure across the school lawn to fertilize

the baby plants. In case you don't know, manure is a nice name for dried-up cow poop, so you can imagine how un-nice it smelled.

"Let's go, Hazel! Quickly, please!" shouted Mrs. Agnes, who was clearly enjoying the fact that she could still boss me around outside school hours. I'd been volunteering in the garden for three days, but it felt like three years. I had moved on from arugula to tomato plants to kale, which rhymes with "wail," which is exactly what I wanted to do at this very—

"Hazel! Manure!"

Well, those were two words I never expected to hear together.

I grumbled and gave the wheelbarrow a shove, the handles slipping out of my sweaty hands. This was so unfair. Elizabeth was having the time of her life at theater camp, Milo was having a ball (literally) at his soccer clinic, The Baby was having a swell time doing baby things, and Mom and Dad were running around in France. Meanwhile, I was *toiling* away at the school garden (which meant I was working hard, and had nothing to do with the bathroom, in case you were wondering).

This would also be a good time to mention I had still found no evidence of the ghost next door. And it's not like I hadn't tried. For the last few nights, as soon as it got dark, I'd sit at my window, aim my binoculars toward the Thibodeauxs' house, and search for signs of anything ghost-like. But other than the porch lights flickering, there was nothing . . . although I did hear the same horrible rattling sounds from time to time, even from my window. If only I could get concrete evidence, like a picture, or a video . . . or plant manure.

Wait, what?

"Manure, Hazel! Now, please!" Mrs. Agnes was shouting. Apparently, I'd gotten caught up in my thoughts and had stopped hauling the wheelbarrow.

I wiped my hands on my shirt, grabbed the handles, and lifted the wheelbarrow back up with a grunt. And then, right as I started to push, I felt prickles and goose bumps. I was getting a tomorrow vision. And even though it wasn't ideal to get a vision while pushing a wheelbarrow full of fertilizer, I was thrilled. Because this could be the vision I was waiting for. The vision that would help me prove there was a ghost next door.

I squeezed my eyes shut and saw . . . a yellow, crinkly circle. Between you and me (and the manure), this was possibly the most boring vision I'd ever had, other than one about a carton of eggs (another long story involving a hill, some sassy fifth graders, and a lecture from Mrs. Agnes about the importance of science lab). The point is, by now I was taking so long, Mrs. Agnes came and took the wheelbarrow from me and began hauling it over herself. It was just as well. That cow-poop smell was making me gag.

14

I'd just finished taking a hot bath, where I had meant to focus on scrubbing off all the garden dirt but instead ended up composing a song about a mermaid named Arugula who ran off to Machu Picchu. I admit, my lyrics could have used some work, but overall it was a pretty good song. Also, I had decided the dirt plastered to my eyebrow would never come off and that there was really no use in trying.

I put on my polka-dotted bathrobe (my new favorite item of clothing) and headed to the kitchen, where I was greeted with a very strange sight. Aunt Jenna was playing some weird song and dancing around the kitchen table. The Baby was doing the same, only with less dancing and more bumping into things and falling over. Milo was there, too, enjoying the entire spectacle.

"Hellllllo, Ha-zyyyyyyy!" Aunt Jenna sang. "We're dancing!"

"I can see that." I giggled. Then I wrinkled my nose. "What's that smell?" I asked.

"It's bibimbap!" Aunt Jenna declared as if it were something I'd actually heard of before. I had not, but from the sound of it I assumed it was either an evil potion from a Disney movie or a disease of the toe.

As it turned out, it was neither of those things. It was a Korean rice dish Aunt Jenna had made for dinner. We all sat down to eat, and

although I was hesitant to try it at first, after one small bite I was hooked. It was delicious. Even The Baby liked it.

Aunt Jenna told us how she learned to make bibimbap on a trip to South Korea, which led Milo to ask what the most popular sport is there, and led me to ask if they ate arugula (answers: soccer, and yes). Then Aunt Jenna started teaching us Korean words and phrases she had learned, and that was a total hoot.

I think my pronunciation was pretty good. Milo's was terrible. And The Baby was still only saying "Doo-doo," so he was way off. It was a pretty fun dinner experience, especially because it got my mind off the ghost. And manure.

The next morning I didn't have to go to the garden. Mrs. Agnes had said she wouldn't need more help for a week or two, when there would be some weeding to do. After Milo took off to his friend's house and I finished the maze on the other box of cereal, Aunt Jenna told me to get dressed because we were going to the playground.

"And what about The Baby?" I demanded to know, troubled that she would consider leaving him here alone. For a moment, I imagined what The Baby would do if he had the entire house to himself (I believed it would include smearing the walls with applesauce and digging through the garbage with Mr. Cheese). Aunt Jenna laughed and said The Baby would be coming with us, which I agreed was a much better plan.

At the playground, The Baby headed straight for the sandbox, where I helped him make a sandcastle that was quite impressive until he started to eat it. (You can't say Mom didn't warn us.) After the swings, the twisty slide, and the swings again, I ran over to the spinny seat that goes around and around so fast you feel dizzy for weeks, or at least several seconds. In between my spins, I  saw a car pull up to the park and then a mother and father helping a toddler out from a car seat. The mother started unloading food from the car and bringing it over to the playground pavilion. I assumed they were setting up for a birthday party. I had been to lots of birthday parties at the park and had fond memories of them all, except for the time my neighbor Jarrod had a piñata and I accidentally whacked the cake off the table with the piñata stick. But other than that, very fond memories.

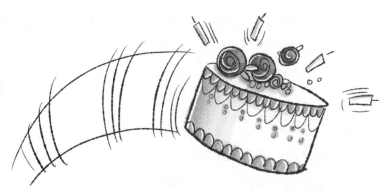

The party guests started to arrive in the form of about five thousand toddlers, so I hopped off the spinny seat (whoa ... so dizzy ...) and headed across the playground, because if you thought one baby was a handful, wait until you experienced millions of them all in one spot.

I found Aunt Jenna and The Baby by the turtle slide.

"Hiya, Hazy!" Aunt Jenna said. "We were just going to the seesaw."

But The Baby didn't seem interested in the seesaw or any other playground equipment, because he was now pointing and squealing and jumping up and down in delight. Then he darted away.

"Sweetie, stop!" Aunt Jenna yelled, and we ran after him.

Naturally, he didn't stop, and soon he was blending in with the gazillion other toddlers and we couldn't see him at all. I'd lost The Baby once before (in my own house—it's a long story involving a loft bed and Bubble Wrap), but never in a park, which was obviously much bigger. This was bad news.

Then Aunt Jenna spotted him. "There he is! At the birthday party!"

We ran over to The Baby, and I could now see what he was after. Tied to the back of a chair was a bunch of brightly colored birthday balloons with smiley faces on them. The Baby was grabbing at them like his little toddler life depended on it.

Aunt Jenna stepped in to gently guide The Baby away. "No, honey, not for you. Say 'Bye-bye, balloons,'" she told him, which immediately triggered a ginormous toddler tantrum.

Aunt Jenna tried to calm him down, but it only got worse. He wanted those balloons, and honestly, I could understand why. After all, a baby is to a

balloon like a bee is to honey, or Elizabeth is to anyone who agrees to watch her tap-dance. The point being, whatever Aunt Jenna was doing wasn't working because The Baby was still screeching his baby head off. And it was giving me a headache. So I did what any normal big sister might do in this situation. I started singing "The Hokey Pokey" to distract him.

"You put your right hand in, you put your right hand out, you put your right hand in, and you shake it all about!"

At first, The Baby just stared at me as if I'd lost my mind. But then, he gave a tiny little smile. And when I spun in a circle and sang, "That's what it's all about," he flat-out started guffawing. Some of the other little kids wandered over with their parents, and before I knew it I was leading an entire group of toddlers in "The Hokey Pokey" right in the middle of the playground. It was kind of fun, and by the fourth round I was really getting into it, adding dance moves and flinging my arms in every direction. Then I spun around a little too fast and fell into one of the moms holding a plate with a piece of birthday cake, getting myself covered

in frosting. Seriously, what was it with this park and cake?

15

It turned out, the nice parents of the birthday child ended up giving The Baby a smiley-face balloon, so my Hokey Pokey shtick was kind of for nothing. But The Baby was thrilled—so thrilled he wouldn't let go of the balloon when we got home. Aunt Jenna attempted to tie the string to a chair, but The Baby kept figuring out how to untie it, which I considered very impressive and also a little bit creepy. I mean, what else could he do that we didn't know about?

After a while, Aunt Jenna gave up tying the balloon to anything, so there

was basically a giant smiley-face balloon bobbing around the house. Personally, I was just
glad it wasn't singing "The Hokey Pokey." That
song had been stuck in my head for hours.

It wasn't until it was almost nighttime that
I realized yesterday's vision hadn't come true
yet. Had I missed seeing something at the park?
On the way home? I knew there was a reason
for every tomorrow vision, so it was important
that I figure it out before "tomorrow" ended,
which was technically "today" because I'd had
the vision "yesterday." The point is, I was now
running all over my house looking for a crinkly
yellow circle.

I started in my room, then made my way to
Milo's room, my parents' room, and then The
Baby's room, where I found a bunch of stuff I
hadn't seen in the longest time—books, balls,
marbles, cards, and an old teddy bear I had
named Aisha.

An hour later, I was sitting on the floor in my room reading *Green Eggs and Ham* to Aisha while bouncing a ball, playing solitaire, and trying to do a magic trick with a marble. I'd found every last thing I could ever imagine. But a crinkly yellow circle? No dice (although I did also find some dice).

I decided to give up on my vision for now. I got up, went over to the window, and picked up my binoculars to look for any new signs of the ghost. Right away, I saw something suspicious.

The window shutters on the front of the Thibodeauxs' house were now open. That was weird because they had been closed before, which was why I'd had to climb up on the ledge.

I kept my binoculars fixed at the window, waiting to see if something else would happen. And then something did. A shadow passed in front of it. I gulped, afraid of what I'd see next. But I couldn't look away.

That's when a one-hundred-percent ghost-like figure appeared in the window.

I screamed at the top of my lungs, threw down my binoculars, and hightailed it out of my room as fast as humanly possible. I ran down the hallway to the living room, looking for

anyone who could protect me. But everyone must already have gone to bed because the living room lights were out and no one was there.

Except for a big round *thing* bobbing toward me.

I screamed and lunged at it, punching it like crazy. When my fists stopped hitting the thing and were just swiping at the air instead, I ran to flip on the light. That's when I saw what I had just attacked. It was The Baby's smiley-face balloon. Which I had just destroyed and was now a big, deflated, wrinkled yellow heap on the floor.

A crinkly yellow circle, you might say.

16

"Can you believe it? I actually saw the ghost!" It was Sunday afternoon, and Elizabeth and I were sitting in my bedroom on the floor.

"No, I cahnt!" Elizabeth replied in a British accent. She had been doing this all week, and although she's pretty good at it, I can't for the life of me understand why she'd need a British accent to play a dancing winged monkey in *The Wizard of Oz*, which takes place in Kansas— or in Oz, at least the monkey part, but then again, since it all turns out to be Dorothy's dream, it does technically take place in Kansas. The point is, I was just happy I had Elizabeth's undivided attention.

"Some . . . wheeeeeeeere over the rainbow . . ."
she started singing.

Or maybe I didn't.

"Elizabeth!" I yelled.

She stopped.

I went on to tell her about my *horrifying*
experience of seeing the *actual ghost* next door.

She began asking questions. "How big was
the ghost?"

"Very big."

"Was it moving around or still?"

"Moving around."

She paused. "Do you think he would like my accent?"

"The *ghost*?" Seriously? I told her it was possible, but we'd never know for sure because I wasn't going near the Thibodeauxs' house ever again, or until I was eighty-eight, whichever came first. But Elizabeth had other ideas.

"Hazy Bloom, you have to go back!"

"Why?"

"Because you are sooo close to solving the mystery! Don't you see? Now we know there really is a ghost!"

"Which means . . ."

"Which means . . ." She narrowed her eyes all mischievous-like. "Now we can get rid of it, once and for all." As much the idea creeped me out, I knew she was right. It was time to get rid of the ghost.

That night, Elizabeth and I made a Ghost

Plan. First, we mapped out a secret route to the Thibodeauxs' house so no one would see us.

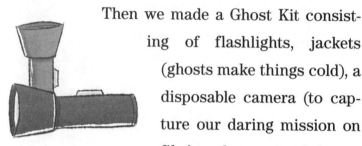

Then we made a Ghost Kit consisting of flashlights, jackets (ghosts make things cold), a disposable camera (to capture our daring mission on film), a foam sword from an old Halloween costume (for protection), and granola bars (in case we needed a snack break). Then we constructed our very own Ghost Detector from an old walkie-talkie, a golf ball, and a magnet shaped like a pineapple. Finally, Elizabeth performed a British rendition of "Ding Dong! The Witch Is Dead," which had nothing to do with the ghost but did, strangely, ease my anxiety.

By bedtime, I was feeling hopeful—and also extremely tired. Working on our

Ghost Plan had exhausted me, and within minutes I was drifting off to sleep . . . until I started to feel the prickles and goose bumps. *Not now,* I pleaded. *No visions.* But it was too late. A vision appeared of green goo, and all of a sudden I was wide awake again.

17

I was peering anxiously out my window, waiting for Elizabeth. She was late, and that was very unlike her.

It was the night of our mission, our Ghost Kit was packed, and I was dressed and ready. We had decided to wear white T-shirts and

pants so the ghost might mistake us for another ghost if we encountered the spirit. Also, we thought it would look kinda cute if we matched.

I scrunched my face against the window, hoping Elizabeth would magically appear. No luck. For a fleeting moment of panic, I wondered if the ghost had gotten her on her way over here. Then I remembered her mom was driving her over and I breathed a sigh of relief. Still, all of this nervous energy was making me jumpy, so while I waited for Elizabeth (who was now thirty-four minutes late), I decided to do some stretches. I wasn't sure what kind of flexibility I'd need to fight a ghost, but it couldn't hurt to warm up my muscles.

I was doing lunges up and down the hallway when Aunt Jenna appeared.

"That's an . . . interesting activity," she commented as I lunged my way past her.

"Why, thank you," I replied.

Aunt Jenna said she'd be putting The Baby down for bed soon and she needed his pajamas from the laundry room. Could I get them?

I didn't want to give away that I was kind of involved with a top-secret Ghost Mission, so I said sure. I raced into the laundry room, grabbed the first pair of baby PJs I could find, ran back, and dumped them on her lap.

"There you go!"

"Thank you—oh, and also his sippy cup?"

I raced to the kitchen to grab his sippy cup. Then she asked me get the baby wipes, lotion, and a diaper. I gritted my teeth. When was Elizabeth going to get here?

Finally, I heard a knock. I grabbed the Ghost Kit and headed to the front door. Then I realized I had grabbed the diaper bag by mistake. I switched it out, thankful that I noticed before it was too late. I wasn't sure how I'd fight a ghost with diaper cream.

I ran to the door and opened it to find Elizabeth standing there. Her face was painted light
blue, there were brown lines all around her
mouth, and she had a black nose.

"Hi there!" she said cheerfully.

"There's something on your face," I pointed out, in case she didn't know.

"It's my winged-monkey makeup!" she said. "We're trying it out for the play. And the funniest thing happened, because the wicked witch was supposed to fly away on her broomstick, but her cape got caught on her cell phone charger, and—"

"Elizabeth!"

"Oh. Sorry." She faced me, all business. "So, are we ready for the Ghost Mission?"

"Ready. Oh, and Elizabeth?"

"Yes?"

"Be on the lookout for green goo," I said.

Elizabeth nodded like that was the most natural thing in the world to hear. This is why I love my best friend: she instantly understood that I was talking about a tomorrow vision. And her winged-monkey makeup looked pretty cool, too.

We carefully checked to make sure no one was looking. Then, like a pair of super-secret superheroes on a super-stealth mission to destroy a ghost, we slipped out the door.

18

We had taken our secret route through my backyard, over the fence, and were now standing at the Thibodeauxs' back door.

"Now what?" I asked her.

"Well, according to our plan," Elizabeth said, "we go inside."

"Inside the house?"

"Well, that is why we're here, Hazy Bloom!"

She was right. I gripped my Ghost Kit and took a deep breath, trying to muster the courage. *You can do this, Hazy Bloom. You are brave. You are strong. You are the wind beneath my wings.* I think that last one was from a song my dad liked to sing and had something to do with the beach, but still, it did the trick. I was feeling inspired. Slowly, I reached for the doorknob.

It was locked. And I have to say, I was kind of relieved, for real live.

"Oh, well . . . we tried. How 'bout we go home and have some pudding?" I said, turning to leave.

"Wait, Hazy. Look!" Elizabeth pointed her flashlight around the side of the house. There was a twisty walkway of flat rocks leading to a sliding door there. I aimed my flashlight to where she was pointing. Splattered on the rocks was a bunch of green stuff. *Green goo.* I shivered.

"Is that what you saw in your vision?" Elizabeth asked, her voice shaky.

133

I nodded. "Do you think it's ghost guts?"

"Ew!" Then she said, "Maybe."

I noticed the sliding door on the side of the house was cracked open a little. We looked at each other and nodded. We went in.

It was dark inside the house, so I turned on my flashlight and beamed it across the room.

"Hello?" I called, as if the ghost would simply come over, shake my hand, and welcome me to the house it was haunting. We tiptoed around to the foyer, near the front door, using my flashlight to guide us. Nothing.

Elizabeth looked frustrated. "Where is it? Where is the ghost?"

"I don't know," I replied. Then it occurred to me that the ghost might have made itself invisible and was possibly *right here, next to me.* I shuddered, trying to decide if I should mention this terrifying thought to Elizabeth. But I never got a chance.

Because that's when we heard footsteps at the side of the house.

I grabbed my foam sword, prepared to spring into action. Out the front windows, I could see the porch lights flickering like crazy. We heard the horrible rattling again. The footsteps were getting closer.

Elizabeth scrunched her eyes shut, as if the ghost wouldn't get her if she wasn't looking at it directly. Meanwhile, I just stood there, frozen in fear. *This is it*, I thought. *I'm about to be eaten by a ghost.* I braced myself for doom.

And then, a perfectly ordinary man wearing overalls and holding two paint cans showed up in the sliding-glass doorway.

I actually wasn't the first one to scream. Neither was Elizabeth. It was the man in the overalls.

He hollered, probably because he didn't expect to see two girls—one waving around a foam sword and the other in winged-monkey makeup—standing in a house he'd thought was

empty. Whatever the reason, it scared him enough that he dropped a paint can on the floor, splattering green paint in all directions, including all over us. I instantly called back my vision.

And I realized it wasn't green ghost goo or ghost guts that I had seen. It was green paint, which meant I had figured out my vision (hooray!). It also was kind of not the point right now.

The man squinted at us, and I fully expected him to scream at us to get out and possibly call the police or, worse, our parents. But he said this instead: "Elizabeth?"

Elizabeth opened her eyes wide. "Mr. Delaney?"

"Um . . . what, now?" I said, because none of this was making sense, for real live.

Elizabeth laughed in surprise, then turned to me. "Hazy, this is Mr. Delaney. He's friends with my mom. He helps out around our house sometimes, when things need to be repaired. He also makes really good oatmeal raisin cookies."

"It's my great-nana's special recipe," the man said with a smile.

As happy as I was that Elizabeth had run into a family friend who enjoyed baking, I did not see how this was helpful to our Ghost Mission. I tugged on Elizabeth's arm to signal it was time to get going. But Elizabeth had turned back to Mr. Delaney.

"What are you doing here? The Thibodeauxs are out of town."

"That's precisely why I *am* here. Mr. and Mrs. Thibodeaux asked me to do some fixin' up around the house while they were away for the summer."

Elizabeth peered out the window. "But where's your car?"

"I live a couple of blocks away. It's easy enough for me to walk over here. I've been coming on the weekends and at night after I get home from my day job. And the Thibodeauxs had all the supplies I needed in their garage. First order of business was the ventilator up in the attic—it's been making a terrible racket."

Ventilator? *The awful rattling sounds.*

"And then I fixed a short in the front room's electrical system. But it is still on the fritz."

Flickering lights.

"But my biggest job has been painting the walls. It's why I've got these drippy paint cans from the garage. And the ladder."

The ladder was propped up against the wall. Behind it, a white sheet was draped over the window—that must have been the "ghost" I saw.

It was a sheet to protect
the window from the paint.
And speaking of paint . . .

"We can help you
clean this up," I said
sheepishly, pointing
to the green splotches
on the bare floor.
"After all, you dropped the paint because of us."

"Luckily, I'm all finished in here and that
can was nearly empty, or we'd have a real situation on our hands. But this is no big deal."

Mr. Delaney gave us some old towels and a
bucket of warm water to clean up the paint. I
felt a huge sense of relief as I realized all of the
things I'd thought were the ghost were actually
from Mr. Delaney fixing up the house. And even
under all that winged-monkey makeup, I could
tell Elizabeth was relieved, too.

"I guess we solved the ghost mystery," she whispered to me.

"Yep. We . . . are . . . good," I said, waving my foam sword in the air, and we giggled.

But we weren't completely out of the woods. As Mr. Delaney opened the door to walk us back to my house, he suddenly looked at us.

"Now it's time for *me* to ask a question. What were you girls doing here in the first place?"

20

"You were so scared," I said to Elizabeth.

"Was not! You were more scared than me. Petrifillized!"

"That's not a word. And also, not true."

Elizabeth and I were eating pudding at my kitchen table. On the way home, we told Mr. Delaney about all of the weird stuff happening at the house that made us think there was a ghost. He shook his head and laughed, saying we have great imaginations and we should never lose that. He also told us that he was done with his work, so we didn't have to worry about any noises, flickering lights, or anything else from a ghost or otherwise. I was glad to hear that.

Especially since I'd decided to give my binoculars to The Baby. Perhaps he can use them to search for more squirrels.

"I guess we should wash this off," Elizabeth said, gesturing to her ankle where some green paint had splattered.

I looked over my shoulder. I hadn't seen Aunt Jenna since we'd gotten back. I assumed she was watching TV in the guest bedroom. But it was definitely a good idea to get cleaned up before she came out and saw the shape we were in.

Elizabeth and I went into the guest bathroom off the hallway, rolled up our pants, and stuck our feet in the tub.

Then I remembered. "Oh no. We never have any soap in here."

"I have some!" Aunt Jenna appeared in the doorway, smiling. In her hand was a bottle of liquid soap and two washcloths. "I bought a brand-new bottle yesterday. Just in case you might need it." Her smile widened. Then she handed me the stuff and headed out the door. She didn't ask where we had been or why we had green paint all over our legs. She just gave me the soap and washcloths and left. As if she knew we would need them.

Now, you try telling me Aunt Jenna doesn't have tomorrow power.

• • • • •

The next morning, Mapefrl was working on a new skateboard trick while I chattered nonstop about the events of the night before.

"And then he opened the door and we were like 'Whoa!' and he was like 'Huh?' and we were like 'You're not a ghost!'" I acted out each part of the story for dramatic effect, although to be honest I wasn't sure why I was telling Mapefrl any of this. I guess I'd kind of gotten used to him being around. Who knows, maybe we would actually end up becoming friends. Then he ruined the moment by talking.

"I can't believe you thought there was

146

actually a GHOST," he said, cracking up. "That's hilarious. Hilarious!"

I think I'd have to settle for "almost friends but still pretty much my annoying classmate" for now.

21

"Let's have a campout!" Aunt Jenna said. "In the backyard. Tonight!"

It was Wednesday, and Mom and Dad were coming home tomorrow. Aunt Jenna had decided she wanted to do something fun for our last official night together.

"Can we pitch a tent?" I asked.

"Of course!"

"And make s'mores?" said Milo.

"Wouldn't be a campout without them."

"Doo doo!" The Baby chimed in, obviously excited about the idea as well.

I couldn't blame him. Who doesn't love a campout? Plus, it was a great way to celebrate our last night with Aunt Jenna. Especially now that I didn't have a ghost to worry about.

Later that morning, we went to the grocery store to buy s'mores ingredients. Then I spent the afternoon making a BLOOM CAMPGROUNDS sign for our campout, a BREAK A LEG card for Elizabeth's performance, a WELCOME HOME banner for Mom and Dad, and a HAZY 4 PRESIDENT sign for myself, just in case I'd need it one day.

During this time, I found myself peeking out the window to see if Mapefrl was outside on his skateboard. I hadn't seen him today. In fact,

I hadn't seen him since yesterday morning, now that I thought about it. Not that I cared.

But he did keep me from being completely bored.

After dinner, Milo helped Aunt Jenna pitch the tent and bring out sleeping bags and pillows while I arranged graham crackers, marshmallows, and chocolate squares on a plate. When it got dark, we headed out back to officially begin the campout. Here's what we did:

1. Took a nighttime nature hike around the backyard.
2. Sang campfire songs (even though we didn't have a campfire), including one The Baby made up that went something like "Doo doo doooooooo, yay! Dooo da da blefhabngoir!"
3. Used our flashlights to make shadow puppets on the tent walls.

4. Looked for Milo's pack of gum that he
   lost on the nature walk.

Finally, it was time for the s'mores. Aunt Jenna
and I went into the kitchen to make them in the
toaster oven. When they were ready, Aunt Jenna
poured some milk for us. While she carried
out the glasses, I grabbed the plate from the

counter, pushed the back door open with my bottom, and then quickly whirled around.

"Presenting the s'mores!" Unfortunately, I did not see that Mr. Cheese was under me, and I tripped right over him (which is technically Dad's job). The s'mores went flying off the plate and scattered all over the grass.

"Ooooooh," The Baby said as if that were some kind of performance I'd put on just for him.

"Look what you did!" Milo scolded me.

"Look what you did!" I scolded Mr. Cheese.

The Baby, meanwhile, had picked up a s'more and started squishing the marshmallow with his fingers, making a gooey mess.

Aunt Jenna giggled at the ruckus and said she'd make a deal with me. If I picked up the s'mores pieces, she'd go inside and make some new ones. And Milo was put on baby-washing duty. Milo scooped The Baby up, and the three of them went inside while I started to clean up the marshmallows and graham crackers before Mr. Cheese got to them. He was sniffing them curiously already.

It was really dark now, so I grabbed my flashlight to spot the marshmallow mess. I was on my last one when I heard something very strange. Like groans. And shrieks. I instinctively glanced over our fence at the Thibodeauxs' house. From our yard we could see the entire top half of their house. The noises were coming from there.

Then the lights in their house started to flicker.

My blood ran cold. *What in the world . . . ?* There was no way. No way this could be happening. Mr. Delaney had said he was done with his work. The Thibodeauxs were still out of town. My mind started racing. Did Elizabeth and I not solve the mystery next door? Was there really a ghost after all?

I stood there frozen for a moment, not knowing what to do. Aunt Jenna was still busy remaking dessert. Milo was still inside washing marshmallow mush out of The Baby's hair. I looked at Mr. Cheese, who honestly seemed up for anything.

"You're coming with me, dude. You were with me when this all started. And you'll be with me when it ends. We're getting this ghost once and for all."

I'm pretty sure Mr. Cheese nodded his approval.

22

As Mr. Cheese and I arrived at the Thibodeauxs' house, the groans and shrieks got louder and the lights were flickering like crazy. Mr. Cheese started barking. I was so scared, I wanted to

turn around and run away. But I didn't. I had faced my fears once already. I could do it again. And this time, I had my dog for backup. I took a deep breath and inched closer to the front door. Then Mr. Cheese started to bark even louder.

"Quiet!" I whispered as he pulled on his leash, yanking my arm around. I made a mental note that if I got out of this alive, the first thing I would do was call a dog trainer, because I was not happy with Mr. Cheese's behavior one bit.

He was now pulling me around the side of the house. The groans and shrieks were getting louder. My heart was beating out of my chest. Mr. Cheese was sniffing around on the ground now, urgently trying to locate something. What was it? Finally, he found what he was looking for. At first, I couldn't tell what it was. But then my eyes adjusted to the dark, and it became clear as day.

It was a cheese puff.

What in the . . .

A few feet away, my eyes landed on a skateboard . . . with a lightning bolt on it. And then . . .

Mapefrl lunged out at me from the side of the house and shouted "Boo!"

I screamed, and fell backward into the grass.

Mapefrl fell to the ground, clutching his sides with laughter. Mr. Cheese was sniffing around him like crazy. I'd like to think he was as furious as I was, but truthfully I think he was just wondering if there were more cheese puffs.

"What are you *doing*, Luke?" I said, my anger rising with every millisecond.

"Playing a prank," he said, still laughing. "And it worked! You totally thought there was a ghost!"

"Did not!"

"Did too!"

"Did not!" I paused. "Fine. I did." Then my curiosity got the best of me. "How did you do all of those creepy things?"

Luke showed me his spooky-sounds machine, a gag gift he'd gotten from the dollar store last Halloween. Then he showed me how he'd used his flashlight to make it look like the lights were flickering. I was sort of impressed. But I had one more question.

"Why did you do this?"

"When you told me there wasn't really a ghost, I knew you would get bored again soon. So I thought I'd keep the excitement going a little longer."

So, he did this . . . for me? That was actually

kind of nice. Really nice, actually. Not that I needed to tell him that.

"I am so mad at you," I said to him, crossing my arms to prove my point.

"Aw, come on. You didn't think it was funny at all?"

"No! Okay, maybe a *little* funny," I said.

"You know what's really funny?" Luke said. "Mr. Cheese likes cheese puffs."

I started laughing. So did Luke. It wasn't the

funniest joke in the world, but for some reason it seemed hilarious. Soon we were laughing so hard our sides hurt.

Then from the other side of the fence, I heard Aunt Jenna muttering, "Where did that girl go now? Ooh, when she gets back here, I'm going to let her ha—"

I looked at Luke. "Gotta go!" When I ran back to the yard with Mr. Cheese, Aunt Jenna was standing with her hands on her hips, her toe tapping the ground. She threw a laser glare at me that was amazingly similar to Mom's. Okay, maybe Aunt Jenna wasn't cheerful *all* the time.

"Hazy Bloom, where did you wander off to, for goodness' sake? I was worried sick!"

"Aunt Jenna, I can explain—" I said, but I was coming up blank. "See, um—"

"It was my fault." Luke poked his head over the fence. "I was playing a trick on her. I got her to come over here."

"Is that true, Hazy?"

I paused. Then I said, "No. It was my decision to go," I told her. "I'm sorry, Aunt Jenna. I shouldn't have left." I said. "But, I felt like . . . I *had* to." I lowered my voice. "To prevent doom. You know . . . as a superhero?"

So here's the thing. When I said that, Aunt Jenna *could* have looked at me like I was crazy. But she didn't. Instead, her angry expression disappeared and she gave me the tiniest little smile. Then she took my hand.

"Let's have some s'mores."

I smiled back. Then I stopped. I turned around. "Luke, do you want a s'more?"

"Uh, sure," he said with a shrug.

It's not that I wanted to hang out with him or anything. I just figured since he went through so much work to play his trick, he might be hungry.

Back at the campsite, we ate s'mores, sang

more songs, and laughed and laughed. Luke even taught us a new game called Campfire Concentration, which was a total blast.

But we all agreed on one thing.

No ghost stories.

23

The next day, Thursday, Aunt Jenna, Milo, The Baby, and I went to see an afternoon performance of *The Wizard of Oz*. I don't know how, but Elizabeth managed to make a dancing winged monkey the most fascinating character in the play. She was fantastic. (And her British accent worked a lot better than I thought it would!)

After the show, I filled Elizabeth in about the entire crazy experience the night before.

"LUKE? Are you serious?"

"Yes!" I laughed, watching her take it all in.

Elizabeth was amazed. And then she told me something else. "You are the bravest person I know."

"I am?"

"Uh-huh. You were going to take on that ghost all by yourself!"

I hadn't thought about it that way. But you know what? She was right! Even though I was scared, I was ready and willing to confront a ghost, and that *was* pretty brave. Next I would have to work on my fear of mice. And smiley-face balloons.

After the show, we all went over to the school so The Baby could play at the playground and eat some sand. Elizabeth came, and I took her to see the school garden. I hadn't been in almost a week, and, to tell you the truth, I kind of missed it.

When we got there I found the section of

arugula I had planted. To my amazement, my arugula plants had grown taller. I guess that's the power of cow poo.

"She's beautiful!" I cooed at the tallest of my plants, and Elizabeth cracked up.

Mrs. Agnes, who was there to put in another bed of herbs, rushed over to say how impressed she was by my gardening skills. And I'd come on the right day. A local reporter was here to do a story on the garden, and he'd like to take a picture of me. How about that? I ended up getting my picture in the newspaper after all!

That evening, Aunt Jenna was making bibimbap again (at my request), while I put together a salad with some baby kale and baby arugula that Mrs. Agnes said I could take.

While we were eating, I heard the front door open. It was Mom and Dad—they were home!

"*Bonsoir!*" my dad said as I leaped into his arms.

"*Dijon!*" I answered, and gave him a big hug.

Mom peppered us all with kisses and asked how our week was.

Milo told her all about his week, and The Baby told his baby version of the same thing.

"What about you, Hazel Basil? How was your week?" Mom asked me as I snuggled into her arms, happy to smell her familiar smell again.

I thought about telling them about the mouse, the ghost, the school garden, Mapefrl, Elizabeth's play, the campout, Mr. Delaney, and me singing "The Hokey Pokey" to a group of toddlers. But there was plenty of time to fill them in. Maybe tomorrow.

"It was awesome," I answered. Because you know what? It actually was.